Dad had a pan.
Floppy ran in.

The pan fell on the mat.

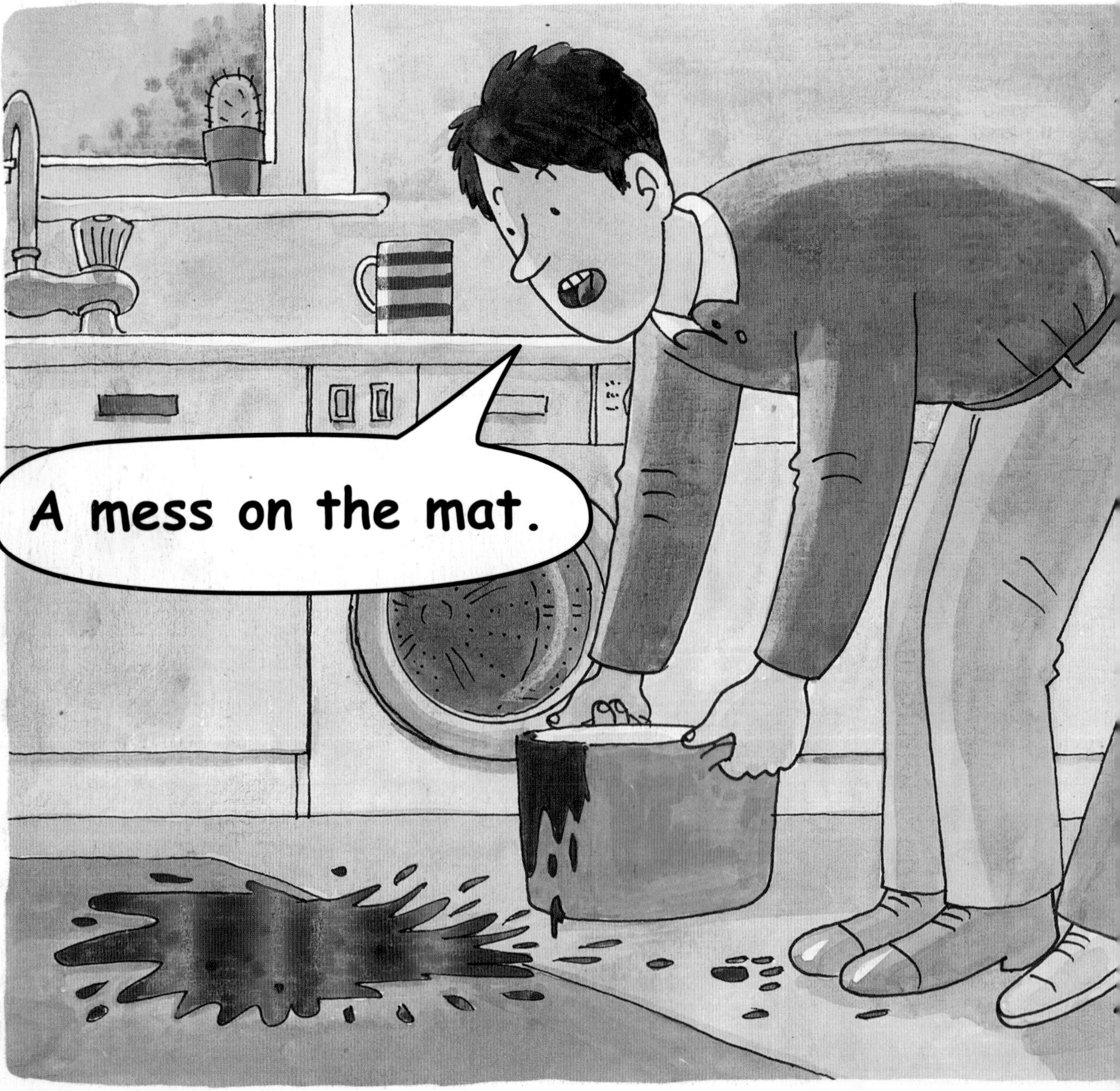
A mess on the mat.

A mess on the dog.
A mess on the rug.

Mum got a mop.

Biff got a rag.

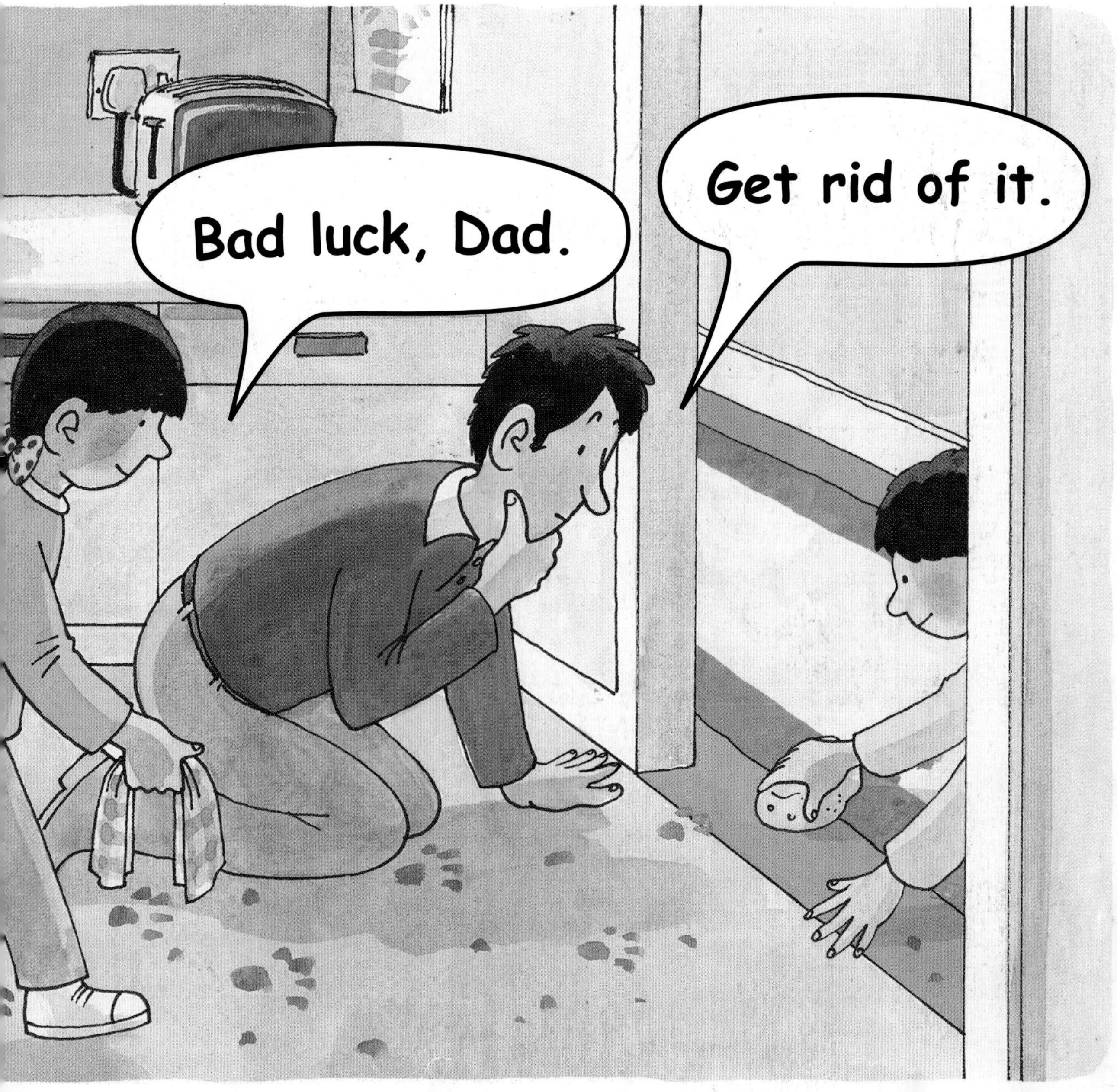
Bad luck, Dad.
Get rid of it.

Dad got a man in.

The man had the kit.

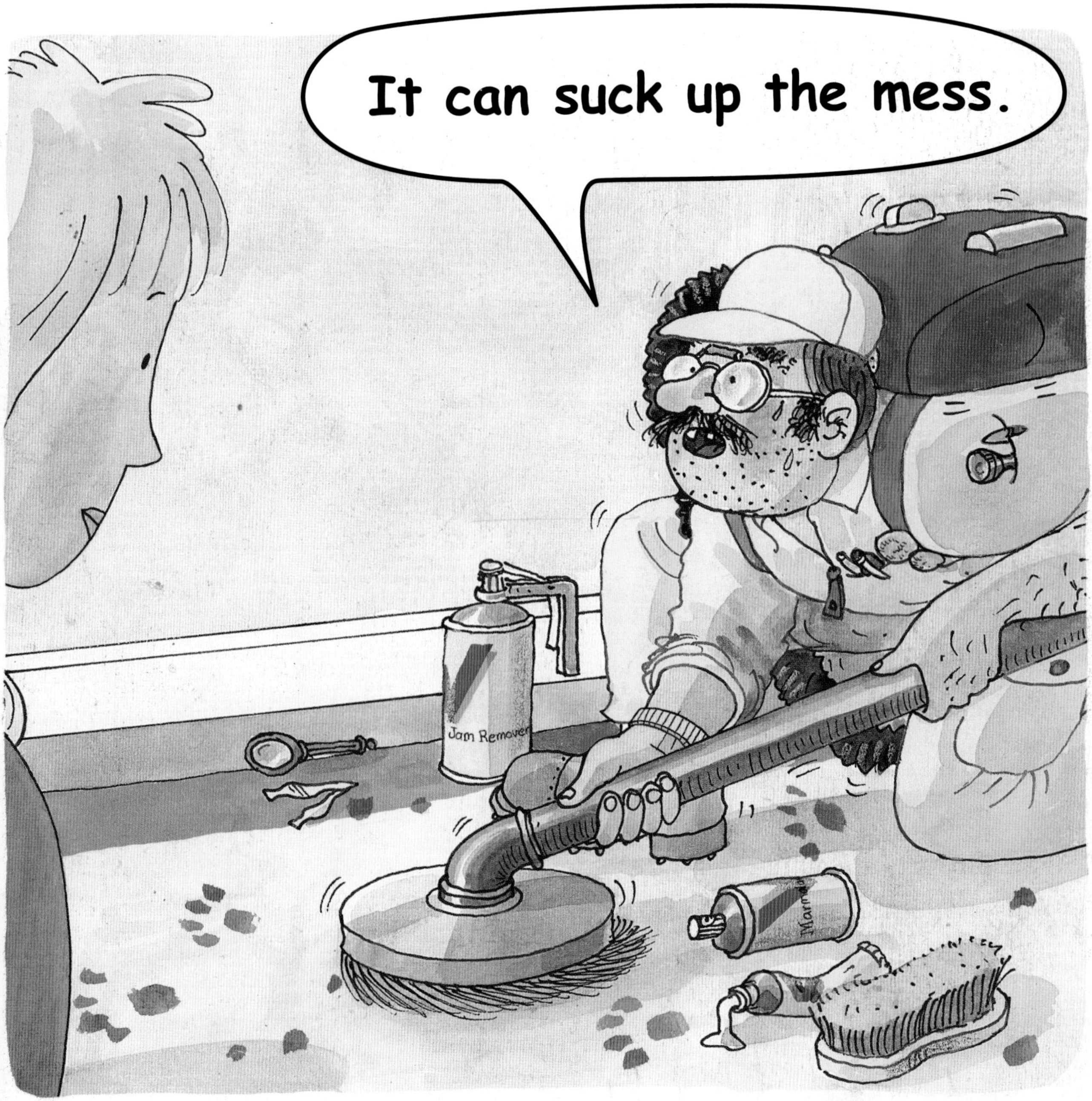
It can suck up the mess.
Jam Remover

The man got rid of the mess.